This is one of a series of books specially prepared for very young children.

The simple text tells the story of each picture and the bright, colourful illustrations will promote lively discussion between child and adult.

British Library Cataloguing in Publication Data

Haselden, Mary
    Going to playgroup.—(Ladybird toddler books.
    Series 833)
    1. Play groups—Juvenile literature
    I. Title   II. Stubbs, Joanna
    372'.216   B1140.2
    ISBN 0-7214-0851-6

First edition

© LADYBIRD BOOKS LTD MCMLXXXV

All rights reserved. No part of this publication may be reproduced, stored in a retrieval system, or transmitted in any form or by any means, electronic, mechanical, photo-copying, recording or otherwise, without the prior consent of the copyright owner.

Ladybird Toddler Books

going to
playgroup

written by MARY HASELDEN
illustrated by JOANNA STUBBS

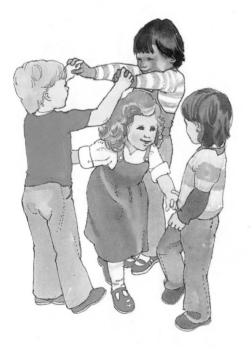

Ladybird Books Loughborough

Today is playgroup day.
In the morning, after breakfast,
the children go to playgroup.

Some girls and boys walk,
others catch a bus,
or ride in a car.

At the hall, the children leave their coats on their pegs.
Some friends are playing already.

Mummy or Daddy says, ''Goodbye!
Have a lovely time.''
Sometimes Mummy may stay to help.

At playgroup there are lots of things to do.
There is sand to play with...

...and water.

This is dough.

These children are rolling the dough
and cutting out shapes.

These boys and girls are painting.
Some children are painting
with their fingers.

In a quiet corner
are some puzzles
and bricks.

There are books to look at.
A helper is reading a story
to some children.

Do you like stories?

These children are dressing up.

These children are playing in the house.

The boys and girls enjoy a drink
together at break time.
They eat a biscuit,
and tell the helpers their news.

After break the children might
make music...

or sing songs together.

The boys and girls enjoy playing
games too.

This helper is gluing with the children.
What are they making?

On this table are some black buttons
and white paper.
What else can you see?

Some children have put things on the
nature table.
Do you know what they are?

At playgroup there are lots of things
to look at and talk about.

These children are sewing.

On fine days the children may play
outside.

It's good to be running outside.

Some days the girls and boys go out for a walk.

Sometimes they go to the park.

Sometimes they go to a farm.

At the end of the morning it's time to tidy up.

Put away the toys.
Sweep up the sand.

Then all the children gather round to listen to a story, or sing some nursery rhymes.

The Mummies and Daddies call to collect the children.

The boys and girls take home the things that they have made.

They have had a happy time!